Katie and the Spanish Princess

James Mayhew

James Mayhew

ORCHARD BOOKS

For a real princess
Vanessa Aduke Olusanya Pearce
(who once longed for a dress like this)
and her family
Mike, Joshua and Chloë
with love

Thanks to Stephen Lennon, Eileen Sheikh and Robert Dukes at the National Gallery, London, for their advice and support. Thanks also to my splendid designer, Clare Mills, and, as ever, to my indispensable editor, Liz Johnson.

ORCHARD BOOKS
338 Euston Road, London NW1 3BH
Orchard Books Australia
Hachette Children's Books
Level 17/207 Kent Street, Sydney, NSW 2000
1 84616 201 7
First published in Great Britain in 2006

A CIP catalogue record for this book is available
from the British Library.
1 3 5 7 9 10 8 6 4 2
Printed in China

Tomorrow was Katie's birthday and Grandma was making a princess costume for her fancy dress party. But the costume didn't look quite right . . .

"We need to see some princess pictures," said Grandma. "Let's go to the gallery."

At the gallery, Katie and Grandma found a picture called *Portrait of the Infanta Margarita* by Diego Velázquez.

"She must be a princess," said Katie. "Look at her dress!"

"It doesn't look very comfy," said Grandma, sitting down.
"Now, I'll just have a quick snooze while you look around."

"It might not be a comfy dress," sighed Katie, "but it *is* beautiful."

"Do you really think so?" said a voice.
Katie looked around, but there was no one there apart from Grandma and she was sound asleep.

"Did you say something?" Katie asked Margarita.
"Yes, but I'm not really supposed to speak," whispered the princess. "Quickly, come inside!"

And she helped Katie into the picture.

“Shall we play together?” asked Margarita. “I’m fed up of being quiet and good, and behaving like a princess.”

“Let’s play dressing up,” said Katie. “I’ll be a princess and you can be a . . . a . . . ”

“I can be you!” cried Margarita. “We’ll swap clothes.”

They quickly changed clothes.
"How do I look?" asked Katie.
"Like a princess!" giggled Margarita. "And now you must behave like one."
"Easy," laughed Katie. "And you have to behave like me!"

"At last, I'm free!" shouted Margarita, jumping into the gallery. Katie found it hard to keep up in the enormous dress. "Wait for me!" she called.

Margarita stopped and waited for Katie to catch up. "Let's look at the pictures," she said. "Which is your favourite?"

"That one," said Katie, pointing to a picture called *Don Manuel Osorio de Zuniga* by Francisco Goya. "Look at all his pets!"

Suddenly, a bird swooped out of the picture, snatched the jewel from the beautiful dress and flew off.

"A magpie!" said Katie.

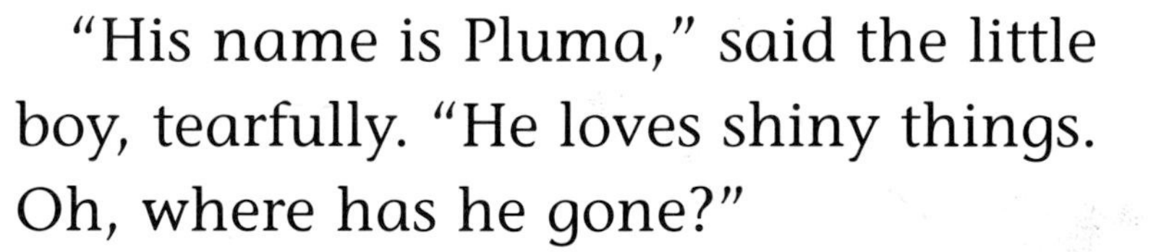

"His name is Pluma," said the little boy, tearfully. "He loves shiny things. Oh, where has he gone?"

"Don't worry, Manuel," said Margarita. "We'll catch him."

"This dress is impossible to run in!" said Katie, as they chased Pluma. But they couldn't catch him and he flew inside another painting.

It was called *The Parasol* by Francisco Goya.
"Come on," said Margarita. "Let's go inside."
And they clambered through the frame.

"Greetings, Your Majesty!" said a young couple with a dog. They thought Katie was the real princess!

"Look, there's Pluma," said Margarita. "He's up in that tree."

"How are we going to catch him?" asked Katie.

"You mustn't climb up in that dress," said the young man. "You'll spoil it."

"Send your servant instead," said the lady, pointing at Margarita.

Margarita climbed up the tree. She was just about to catch the bird when the dog jumped up and started barking. Pluma flew off into the gallery.

"Come on, Margarita!" said Katie. "Follow that bird!"

"What a strange princess," said the lady.

There was no sign of Pluma in the gallery, but they could hear someone laughing. It was a scruffy little boy in a painting.

"*A Peasant Boy Leaning on a Sill*," read Margarita, "by Bartolomé Murillo."

"Are you looking for a bird?" asked the boy. "It flew in here."

So Margarita and Katie squeezed through the small frame.

They found themselves in the ruins of an old house. Pluma was perched high up in a window, and they couldn't reach him.

"I've got an idea," whispered the boy. He broke up a piece of bread and threw the crumbs on the floor. "It's the last of my food, so I hope it works."

Pluma spotted the bread and flew down. In a flash, the boy caught the bird and handed the jewel back to Katie.

"Thank you," said Katie. "It was kind of you to use your bread to catch Pluma."

The boy bowed and said, "You're welcome, Your Majesty."

“Manuel will be worried about Pluma,” said Margarita, taking the bird. “We should go.”

“That poor boy must be very hungry,” said Katie, waving goodbye.

“Yes,” said Margarita. “We always have plenty of food, so I suppose I’m lucky being a princess, really.”

They walked back to Pluma's picture, where Manuel was waiting anxiously.

"You found him!" he said, stroking Pluma gently.
"Make sure you hold onto his ribbon," said Katie.
"I will," said Manuel. "Thank you!"

Suddenly they heard a loud voice.
"MARGARITA, where are you?"
"Oh, it's Papa!" said Margarita.
Katie saw a tall man in a painting called *Philip IV of Spain in Brown and Silver* by Diego Velázquez. "Goodness me!" she gasped. "A real king!"

"I'm here, Papa," said Margarita.

"Heavens, what are you wearing?" said the king. "And who is this other little princess?"

"This is my friend, Katie," said Margarita. "We swapped clothes so she could be a princess for the day!"

Katie ran back and finished her lemonade.
"Come on," said Grandma. "Let's go home and make that princess costume."
"That's very kind," said Katie. "But I don't think I want to be a princess any more . . . I want to be a pirate, instead!"

The Spanish School of Artists

VELÁZQUEZ (1599-1660)

The greatest thing a Spanish painter could wish for was to become a court artist for the king, and to paint portraits of the royal family. Diego Rodriguez de Silva y Velázquez was perhaps the greatest court artist of all time, and is believed by many to be the best portrait painter the world has ever known. Velázquez was born in Seville in 1599, and aged ten began to train to become an artist. In those days, training took many years, but Velázquez was only twenty-four when King Philip IV made him his court artist. Velázquez's brushstrokes seem to capture not only the wonderful expressions of the people he painted, but also a striking contrast between dark and light – an influence which can be seen in the paintings of many artists to this day.

Portrait of the Infanta Margarita – 'Infanta' is the Spanish word for princess. King Philip IV sent portraits of his daughter, Margarita, to Austria, where his wife, Mariana, came from.

Philip IV of Spain in Brown and Silver – The king looks very splendid in his fine clothes, but take a closer look at his face. What expression do you think Velázquez has managed to show, and what might the king be thinking?

MURILLO (1617-1682)

Bartolomé Esteban Murillo was also born in Seville, but was never made a court artist. Murillo still became famous and much admired for his religious paintings and his pictures filled with happy, laughing children.

A Peasant Boy Leaning on a Sill – Murillo liked to paint the ordinary poor children of Seville. Perhaps he thought they had more fun than the rich people in fine clothes.

GOYA (1746-1828)

Francisco José de Goya y Lucientes was born in a little village in Aragon. His family were poor, but he worked hard and eventually became a court artist for King Charles IV. He didn't just paint portraits, and some of his pictures were sad because Spain went to war. Goya's last works were more decorative, and influenced later French art.

The Parasol – This was the plan for a tapestry for the Royal Palace in Madrid.

Don Manuel Osorio de Zuniga – As well as painting the king, Goya painted portraits for other rich families. Manuel was the son of a count.

Perhaps if you ever visit Spain you will see the castles and palaces where the real Margarita and her family once lived.

Acknowledgements:

Portrait of the Infanta Margarita (1651-73) Aged Five, 1656 (oil on canvas), Velázquez, Diego Rodriguez de Silva y (1599-1660)/Kunsthistorisches Museum, Vienna, Austria/Bridgeman Art Library; Don Manuel Osorio de Zuniga c.1788-9 (oil on canvas), Goya y Lucientes, Francisco José de (1746-1828)/Metropolitan Museum of Art, New York, USA/Bridgeman Art Library; The Parasol, 1777 (oil on canvas), Goya y Lucientes, Francisco José de (1746-1828)/Prado, Madrid, Spain/Bridgeman Art Library; A Peasant Boy Leaning on a Sill, 1670-80 (oil on canvas), Murillo, Bartolomé Esteban (1617-82)/National Gallery, London, UK/Bridgeman Art Library; Philip IV (1605-65) of Spain in Brown and Silver, c.1631-2 (oil on canvas), Velázquez, Diego Rodriguez de Silva y (1599-1660)/National Gallery, London, UK/Bridgeman Art Library